SHARING THE LOVE OF BIRDS

Tea with Lady Sapphire

Carl R. Sams II & Jean Stoick

Acknowledgements

*W*e would like to thank our loyal staff: Karen McDiarmid, Becky Ferguson, Kirt Manecke, Bruce Montagne, Sandy Higgins, Denise & Lanny Caverly, Mark & Deb Halsey and Nancy Higgins. Special thanks to Rose Noor (the cookie lady and mitten maker).
Thanks to Jim Berry and the Roger Tory Peterson Institute, Catherine McClung, Julie Craves, Bridget Llewellyn, Laura Sams, Robert Sams, Ron & Diane Sams, Hugh McDiarmid, and Tom & Lisa Nyenhuis for their contributions.
Thank you Gary Keyes, K Westin, and Michelle & Larry Roderick for helping us locate pileated woodpeckers to photograph.
Thank you Grandma Ellie Olszewski, Dawn Gulich, Caroline-Daisy Gulich, Lainey-Marie Gulich, Heiner Hertling, Heidi Hertling, Paige Ducharme & Hannah Ducharme for sharing hot chocolate and feeding the birds.
Thanks to Greg Dunn of Digital Imagery for his color expertise.

Publisher:
Carl R. Sams II Photography, Inc.
361 Whispering Pines • Milford, MI 48380
800/552-1867   248/685-2422   Fax 248/685-1643
www.strangerinthewoods.com
www.carlsams.com

Karen McDiarmid – Art Director

Sams, Carl R.
Tea with Lady Sapphire: Sharing the Love of Birds
by Carl R. Sams II & Jean Stoick, Milford, MI
Carl R. Sams II Photography, Inc. © 2011

Summary: A grandmother shares her love of birds
and nature with her grandchildren.

Printed and bound June 2011 – #65587
Friesens of Altona, Manitoba, Canada

ISBN 978-0-9827625-1-6
Winter Birds (Nature / Winter)
For children of all ages.

Library of Congress Control Number: 2011907347

10 9 8 7 6 5 4 3 2 1

For those who protect wild places and
care for our feathered friends.

Sweet Child gazed out the window
making circle clouds
on the cold glass
with her breath.

Swirling snowflakes covered
the grass and fell thick
onto the trees that
began the woods.

Her grandma was right.
It was a perfect snow . . .
a packing snow.

The morning sun came up gifting them with
a crystal white snow globe world.

The phone jangled!

"We have a mission, Sweet Child,"
Gram's voice sang out.

"Our feathered friends
are expecting us.
And as you know,
a do-er's deed
must be done.

Bring Little Squirt
and make sure
he is hatted-up.

We need to
get on with
his education."

With chatter
and laughter and brightly
colored mittens,
they shaped their snowman
just outside the
breakfast window.

The three of them filled
an old floppy-eared hat
with nuts and seeds
and placed it on the snowman's head.

Gram planted
a fallen birch log
into the snow and
stuffed the cavities with suet.

The last
of the feeding stations
was complete.

Job well done!

"Look who's here already!
It's our upside-down bird,
the white-breasted nuthatch!"
Sweet Child
pointed out.

"This is our tradition,
Little Squirt,"
nodded Gram pouring her tea.

"Welcome to our club!

Tut-tut-tut . . . Mr. Tut!
Those snickerdoodle cookies
are *not* for you."

"Winter is a difficult season
    and we take care of our
    feathered friends,"
    Gram explained.

"Keep an eye out
for our Lady Sapphire.

She'll land on the old hemlock
    looking for bugs and beetles.

She is a pileated woodpecker . . .
    a *very* large woodpecker."

Mr. Tut's tail twitched and thumped
on his special perch
as the first guest flitted in.

The chickadee flew
his crooked path
to land on the
snowman's nose.

"There's Mama's *favorite* bird,
the chickadee-dee-dee!"
Squirt grinned.

"Yes," Gram agreed,
"and he's the friendliest
of all the birds.
It's no surprise
that he's first to greet
our snowman."

"Look at that red bird!"
chirped Squirt.

"He's the male cardinal,
and such a show-off red,"
Gram replied.
"The male birds
are usually
the flashy ones."

"And those blue jays are bold as brass!" Gram exclaimed.

"Some people think they are bullies," said Sweet Child.

"Yes, but they have a job to do,"
continued Gram.
"The jays will sound an alarm,
warning all the birds
when a hawk soars above."

Sweet Child smiled at
the tufted titmouse.
"His wings are like an angel's,"
she whispered.

"Oh look!
A woodpecker!
Is that her? Is that Lady Sapphire?"
interrupted Squirt.

"No . . . not yet, Squirt.
That's our red-bellied woodpecker,
with red on her head
but only a touch
on her belly,"
Gram smiled.

"O-o-ooh . . . I see the red on her belly!"
piped up Little Squirt.
"I'm really good at this!"

"I know you are!
You have eyes like an eagle,"
said Gram.

"And look!"
Sweet Child pointed out.
"There's my tufted titmouse.
He looks so different when he's
perched on a branch."

"It's the berry bandits!"
    sang out Sweet Child.

A flock of smooth feathered
    cedar waxwings glided in
and landed on a
    snowdrift crab tree.

"They'll pluck all
those berries in no time,"
Gram told them.

On a lower branch
hung a thistle feeder
with many perches.

"Thistle is the goldfinches'
favorite treat,"
Sweet Child
explained.

"Mr. Goldfinch wears his
olive-brown coat during
winter instead of his
summer yellow,"
added Gram.

"Look closely!
The hairy and downy woodpeckers
are *almost* alike,"
Gram noted.

"The hairy is
much bigger than
the little downy.

And look at
the hairy's red cap.
That's how you can tell
it's a male.

The ladies don't wear
a red cap."

A red-breasted nuthatch
landed on the hat,
as a little red squirrel
stole another nut
from the
snowman's face.

We watched him take
one nut,
and then another . . .
until there were
none.

"That nut thief
will keep us busy
replacing nuts all day long!"
laughed Gram.

"Is *that* Lady Sapphire, Grammy?"
Squirt called out,
as a new visitor snatched
a kernel of corn.

"Not yet," she answered.
"That's our red-headed woodpecker
and he's a rare one!

Good spot!"

A trio of crows
watched from above.

"The crows like corn too,"
added Sweet Child.

The gentle mourning doves
and grey juncos
pecked at scattered
corn and seed.

Even the turkeys
strutted by in their slow step
to gobble up seeds.

"There's Lady Sapphire!
That polka-dotted bird!"
hooted Squirt.

Gram chuckled,
"That's the flicker.
Sometimes they come to the feeder,
but they'd rather have bugs."

"I like bugs too," smiled Squirt.

The jays were resting
in the snowy branches
when a large shape swooped
down from the treetops.

"Who-ooo-ooa!"
shouted Squirt,
pointing at the tall evergreens
on the edge of the woods.

"Look at *that* big bird!"

"It's *her!* It's Lady Sapphire . . .
in for a landing!"
Gram laughed.

"And look!
There's a *second* pileated woodpecker
waiting for her on the tree.
Do you see him?

Now *that's not*
your mama's chickadee!"
Gram crowed.

"Pick up your binoculars.
Do you see
his red mustache?

Can you see the difference?"

"Lady Sapphire has a mate!

It's time for a toast!

Raise your teacups and
welcome Mr. Succotash
with his handsome
red mustache."

"Welcome, friends!

Welcome
to our backyard!"

"How long will we feed the birds?"
Squirt asked.

Sweet Child answered
just the way
Gram would . . .

"Until the frogs
sing and
the trees
grow new leaves."

Their snowman came and went.

And like always,
they would wait
for the next
perfect snow.

"We will meet again . . .
my little circle of friends.

It's our tradition and our duty,"
Gram explained,
tipping Mr. Tut
from his chair.

"Raise your teacups
to our feathered
friends!"

Pileated
Woodpecker
female

Hairy
Woodpecker
male

Northern
Flicker
male

Red-headed
Woodpecker

Downy
Woodpecker
male

Red-bellied Woodpecker
male

White-
breasted
Nuthatch

Red-breasted
Nuthatch

American Goldfinch
winter

Mourning
Dove

Black-capped
Chickadee

Tufted
Titmouse

American
Goldfinch
*male in
summer*

Northern
Cardinal
male

Northern Cardinal
female

American Crow

Cedar
Waxwing

Blue Jay

Common
Redpoll
female

Dark-eyed Junco
male

Fox
Squirrel

White-tailed
Deer

Red
Squirrel

House
Mouse

Wild Turkey
female

Spoiled
House Cat
Mr. Tut

Gram's Amazing Snickerdoodles

Cream together: 1-1/2 c sugar, 2 large eggs, 1/2 c butter, 1 tsp vanilla

Mix together: 3/4 c flour, 1 tsp baking soda, 1/4 tsp salt, 1/2 tsp ginger,
2 tsp cream of tartar, 1/2 tsp nutmeg

1. Combine dry ingredients into creamed mixture.
2. Shape into balls about the size of a walnut.
3. Roll them around in a bowl with a mixture of
   2 tbsp sugar and 2 tbsp cinnamon.
4. Place 2 inches apart on an
   ungreased cookie sheet.
   Bake 375°   8-10 min.

Don't wait for them to cool.
Dunk them into milk or hot chocolate . . .
   so scrumptious!

When your Sweet Child asks for another . . .
look sternly with hands on your hips,
stomp your feet and say . . .
"Absolutely not!
   Take THREE!"

When they have grown, they will
tell that story, with a warm smile,
   again and again.

Hey wait!
That's <u>2</u>-3/4 cups
of flour!